The ENORMOUS SNORE

Text by **M. L. MILLER**

Illustrations by **KEVIN HAWKES**

G. P. Putnam's Sons ‣ **New York**

For Sandy—M. L. M

To all those who snore and won't admit it—K. H.

Text copyright © 1995 by M. L. Miller. Illustrations copyright © 1995 by Kevin Hawkes
All rights reserved. This book, or parts thereof, may not be reproduced in any form
without permission in writing from the publisher. G. P. Putnam's Sons, a division of
The Putnam & Grosset Group, 200 Madison Avenue, New York, NY 10016. G. P. Putnam's Sons,
Reg. U.S. Pat. & Tm. Off. Published simultaneously in Canada. Printed in Hong Kong
by South China Printing Co. (1988) Ltd.
Book designed by Gunta Alexander. Text set in Schneidler.

Library of Congress Cataloging-in-Publication Data
Miller, M. L. The enormous snore / by M. L. Miller; illustrated by Kevin Hawkes. p.   cm.
Summary: A young girl cures the king of his deafening snore by having his bed moved
to Echo Ravine. [1. Snoring—Fiction. 2. Echo—Fiction. 3. Kings, queens, rulers, etc.—Fiction.]
I. Hawkes, Kevin, ill. II. Title. PZ7.M627En   1995 [E]—dc20   93-42396   CIP   AC   ISBN 0-399-22650-8

1 3 5 7 9 10 8 6 4 2

First Impression

Letty and her family had been traveling for days through the mountains, looking for a new home. Then they became separated in a storm.

When the storm was over, Letty stood alone calling for her mother and father, only to hear her words echo straight back at her.

For hours Letty wandered hopelessly, until she heard a strange rumbling noise from down in the valley.

It sounded like a volcano erupting. The earth began to tremble, and the sound rolled through the land. Doors rattled on their hinges, and plates on their shelves. People ran outside in total confusion. For that was the night the King started to snore.

Letty followed the sounds to the castle. There she bumped into the Royal Seamstress, who was shaking her fist at the King's tower.

"Enough!" the Royal Seamstress shouted. "Take these and embroider them for the Queen!" She handed Letty the royal curtains and ran off with her hands over her ears.

Letty was still lost, but at least she had a place to spend the night. Soon she would start looking for her family.

Upstairs in the castle, the King could not be roused from his sleep. The Queen tried everything she could think of, but nothing worked, and so she just had to wait for him to wake up in the morning.

The next day Letty listened to the biggest
brains in the country trying to decide what to do.
And that night under the King's mattress they
hid a pea, a turnip, and an artichoke to keep him
from sleeping soundly.

Letty began to have an idea of her own. She got
to work embroidering the Queen's new curtains.

That next night *again* the King snored even louder than before. Apples fell from trees, and birds flew south. People cringed beneath blankets or huddled together in basements or covered their ears with pots.

Letty stitched and stitched.

At twilight she carefully hung the new curtains and tied them back with a ribbon.

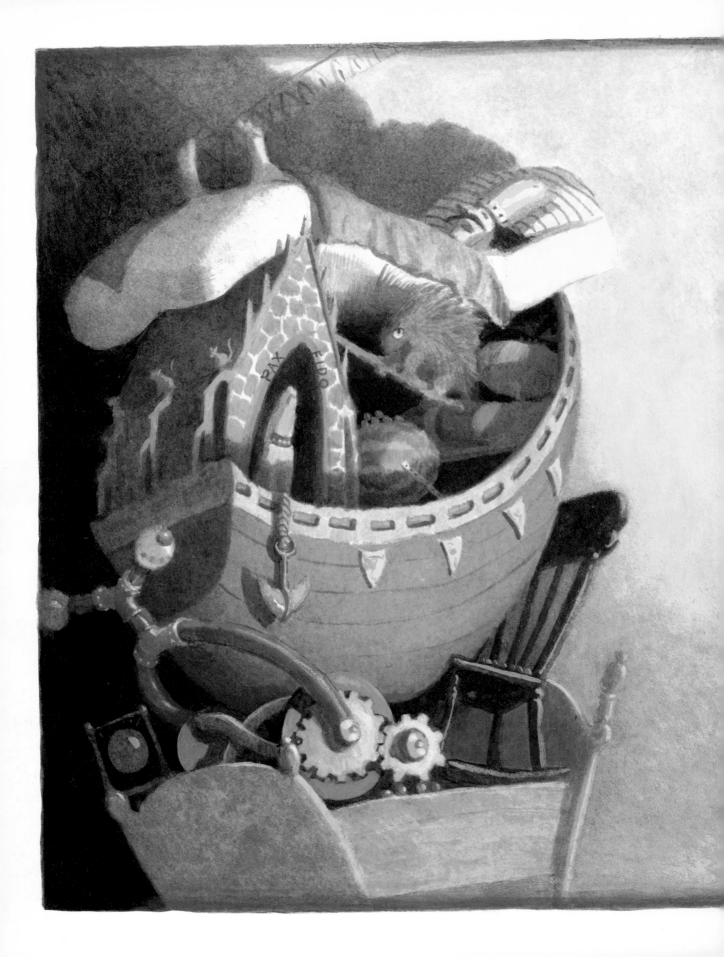

The next day, the biggest brains hid three radishes, a pound cake, and a watermelon; four walnuts, a dinner gong, and a lawn mower; five sesame seeds, a piccolo, and a doghouse; six peach pits, a porcupine, and a rowboat; seven jelly beans, a sledgehammer, and a rocking chair under the King's mattress.

But by midnight, *again* he started to snore, and the sound was deafening! Enemy soldiers invading the country in the dark thought it was a secret weapon, and ran away in panic.

On went the snore, and on.

The next evening when Letty drew the royal curtains, the Queen had a sudden inspiration.

In a midnight procession the King's bed was carried up the mountain. Letty trailed behind, exhausted by all that stitching.

At last they came to the place known as Echo Ravine. There the royal bed was put safely down.

It was *then* that His Majesty let out the snore of all snores—which thundered down the ravine, then came echoing straight back.

The noise was so dreadful that the King sat straight up in bed, shocked, gasping for breath. Everyone was sure he would be cured of his snoring forever!

And as the royal bed was carried back down the mountain, the King's attendants yanked all the objects from under the King's mattress to lighten the load. The farther down they marched, the farther Letty fell behind, growing wearier and wearier, until she could hardly keep her eyes open. The King, however, was comfortable, and soon he fell into a very deep sleep. He slept like a rock and, for a change, made not a peep.

Just before dawn a poor family came over the peaks, searching for their lost daughter.

Then, as if by magic, they began to find wonderful things all along the road to help them make a new home: three radishes, a pound cake, and a watermelon; four walnuts, a dinner gong, and a lawn mower; five sesame seeds, a piccolo, and a doghouse; six peach pits, a porcupine, and a rowboat; seven jelly beans, a sledgehammer—

and a rocking chair, just the right size
for Letty, tipping in the breeze.